Princess Mar
The Moon Thieves

A bilingual multimedia tale
To access the audio accompaniment please visit:
http://wp.me/P4K7oZ-o2 or scan the code

Foreword

Princess Marisol & Moon Thieves is the book we have all been waiting for. As a mother and a sociologist, I am thrilled that Princess Marisol & Moon Thieves embodies the diversity and beauty of our country and world. I believe we can all learn from embracing our multi-racial, multi-cultural and diverse worldviews and experiences. Come and walk with Princess Marisol and walk in beauty.

---

*Dr. Nancy Lopez, is an Associate Professor of Sociology at the University of New Mexico. Dr. Lopez serves as the Director and Co-founder of the Institute for Study of "Race" & Social Justice, **RWJF Center for Health Policy** at the University of New Mexico.*

Dedication:
This book, like my life's work, is dedicated to you my beautiful daughter **Marisol Paramo**, the Princess of my soul. You are my inspiration for this story, which overflows with my love for you.

For:
This book is for my mom, **Lucy Salazar**. For all the hard work, countless hours and dreams that you sacrificed in order to raise me and my brothers, this book serves as a testament to my appreciation of you.

Thanks:
I would like to thank my wonderful life-partner, **Yvette Sandoval**. Her innumerable hours of dedicated work, in every facet of the production of this project, were invaluable and unforgettable. I owe her much more than thank you and I love you, but that's what I have to give from the innermost depths of my heart.

At sunset, out of the mists, arose the mighty Sea Empress. On the horizon, where the sun meets the sea, the great Sun King emerged from the rays to greet her. On this day, it was predestined that the moon and tides would entwine them forever.

Al atardecer la majestuosa emperatriz del mar se asomó entre la neblina. Sobre el horizonte, donde el sol se topa con el mar, el gran Rey Sol extendió sus rayos para saludarla. Quedó predestinado ese día que la luna y la marea los uniría para siempre.

Over many centuries together, beneath the light of many moons, their love for one another grew. One spring morning, when the day was as long as the night, the Sea Empress surfaced from between the waves at dawn, and tenderly placed a giant clam on the warm sand.

Juntos compartieron la luz de muchas lunas a lo largo de muchos siglos, y así creció el amor que se tenían uno hacia el otro. Una cierta mañana primaveral, durante uno de esos días que duran tanto como la noche, la Emperatriz del mar se asomó por entre el oleaje del alba, y delicadamente colocó una almeja gigante sobre la tibia arena.

Suddenly, under the warm gaze of the Sun King, the clam opened to reveal a gift from the sun and sea. As Princess Marisol cooed playfully, Alessa, a curious young sea otter, slowly crept towards the clam. Alessa the otter had been chosen to be Princess Marisol's protector.

De repente, bajo la mirada fija y cálida del Rey Sol, se abrieron las conchas de la almeja, dejando al descubierto aquel regalo del sol y la mar. Mientras su hija murmullaba suave y juguetona, se acercaba lentamente Alessa, una curiosa y joven nutria marina. Alessa había sido escogida para ser la protectora de la princesita Marisol.

Princess Marisol spent her days on her secluded island home, playing hide-and-seek with Alessa and other island creatures, building castles made of sand, and collecting seashells and trinkets washed onto the shore by the sea.

La princesa Marisol pasaba sus días en su remota isla, jugando a las escondidas con Alessa y otras criaturas marinas, construyendo castillos de arena y coleccionando conchas de mar y otros cachivaches que la espuma del mar arrastraba hasta la playa.

When the evening sun sank below the waves, Princess Marisol would slip back into the sea. Once in a while, as she wandered to the shore at dusk, she would wonder what life was like beyond the horizon. Every night, she fell asleep to the soft, beautiful melodies that emanate from the moon.

Cuando el sol del crepúsculo se escondía bajo las olas, Marisol se sumergía en la profundidad del mar. Mientras deambulaba por la costa al atardecer, a veces se preguntaba cómo sería la vida más allá de los confines del horizonte. Todas las noches se dormía al son de suaves y bellas melodías provenientes de la luna.

On the other side of the horizon, upon a sea of sand, two spirited musicians crafted sounds into music. Juancho with his bass guitar and Mato with his drum, journeyed from town to town and village to village, sharing their gift of music with everyone, everywhere they went.

Al otro lado del horizonte, sobre un mar de arena, dos músicos animados y llenos de vida creaban música y sonidos. Juancho, con su bajo y Mato con su tambor, viajaban de pueblo en pueblo y de ciudad en ciudad, compartiendo su don para la música con todos.

One particular dawn, as their last devoted friend wearily drifted off to meet the day, Juancho, the prankster, laid down his bass guitar and called to the moon, pleading with her to stay. Meanwhile, the ever-clever Mato sat quietly thinking and fiddling with his drum. Suddenly, Mato hatched a plan that would allow them to play forever! They would STEAL THE MOON!!

Un cierto amanecer, mientras su último fiel seguidor se retiraba para iniciar el día, Juancho el bromista, hizo a un lado su bajo y le hizo un llamado a la luna, suplicándole que se quedara. Mientras tanto, el ingenioso Mato, pensaba en silencio mientras toqueteaba su tambor. Y de pronto, se le ocurrió un plan que les permitiría seguir tocando sin interrupción! Se iban a ROBAR LA LUNA!

Long ago, Mato had heard a myth that the moon could be lured with music, so they set off in search of the moon. The Moon Thieves found themselves on the other side of the world, on Princess Marisol's beach, and they eagerly began to play to the moon. Intrigued, the moon drew nearer and nearer, becoming smaller and smaller. Without warning, Juancho snatched the moon from the night sky. Through the black of night, Juancho and Mato triumphantly scampered off. Little did the Moon Thieves know, Alessa the otter was a witness to their misdeeds.

Hace mucho tiempo, Mato oyó decir que era posible encantar a la luna con los sonidos de la música. Los Robalunas decidieron lanzarse en busca de ella, y pronto se hallaron al otro lado del mundo, en la playa de la Princesa Marisol, y ansiosamente empezaron a tocar enérgicamente. La luna, intrigada, se acercó lentamente, haciéndose más y más chica. De pronto y sin advertencia, Juancho arrancó la luna del cielo nocturno. Bajo el manto oscuro de la noche, Juancho y Mato, triunfantes, se dieron a la fuga. No se imaginaban que la nutria Alessa había presenciado sus fechorías.

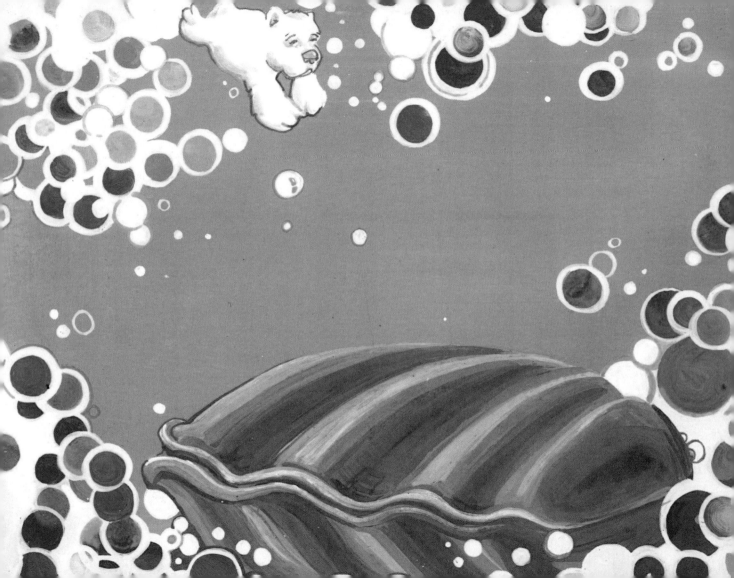

Alessa scurried to the shore, plunged down to the ocean floor, and roused Princess Marisol from her sleep. The otter told Princess Marisol that two musicians, the Moon Thieves, had stolen the moon and were headed to the mainland on their way to the other side of the world! Together, they hastily swam to the surface and discovered mystified stars in a moonless sky!

Alessa salió disparada hacia la orilla, se sumergió al el fondo del mar, y despertó a la princesa Marisol. La nutria de mar le comentó a la princesa que dos músicos, los Robalunas, se habían robado a la luna, e iban camino a tierra firme, dirigiéndose hacia el otro lado del mundo! Juntas, nadaron apresuradamente a la superficie y observaron las estrellas desconcertadas en un firmamento sin luna!

At dawn, Alessa urged Princess Marisol to come ashore. As sunlight spread throughout the sky, ocean waves splashed and crashed in every direction. Once on land, Princess Marisol searched for comfort in her favorite island hiding place. Alessa followed her there and whispered, "Please Princess Marisol, you must do something." The Princess and the otter now knew that the capture of the moon had upset the calm ocean.

Al amanecer, Alessa le insistió a la princesa Marisol que la acompañara a la orilla de la playa. Mientras la luz del sol comenzaba a iluminar el cielo, las olas del mar salpicaban y se estrellaban en todas direcciones. Al llegar a la playa, Marisol acudió a la comodidad de su escondite favorito en la isla. Alessa la siguió hasta allí y susurró, "Por favor Princesa Marisol, tienes que hacer algo". La princesita y la nutria ahora sabían que la captura de la luna había alterado la tranquilidad de la mar.

Princess Marisol was hesitant to leave her island, for never in her eight years had she ever left its shelter. Despite her reluctance, Princess Marisol knew she had been chosen for this quest. With a kiss from her mother, the Sea Empress, and with the rays from her father, the Sun King, to light the way, the Princess and the otter set off on the longest day, across the island, towards the mainland to rescue the moon.

Durante sus ocho primaveras, Marisol nunca había abandonado la comodidad de su isla. Se sentía indecisa e insegura sobre la decisión, sin embargo sabía que era la persona escogida para esta misión. Marisol y su nutria emprendieron viaje el día más largo del año, partiendo desde la isla hacia tierra firme, con el fin de rescatar a la luna. Su madre, la Emperatriz del Mar, se despidió con un beso y su padre el Rey Sol, le iluminó el camino con sus rayos.

Meanwhile, the Moon Thieves with the captured moon in tow, were traveling the world entertaining old friends and new friends with their tunes. Each night, they would release the moon, whereupon he would rise slightly, but not too high and never too bright, for he was captivated by their music.

Mientras tanto los Robalunas, con la luna secuestrada, viajaban por el mundo, deleitando con su música a viejos y nuevos amigos. Por las noches, dejaban suelta a la luna, quien se elevaba levemente, pero nunca muy alto y sin relucir demasiado, pues sentía el encanto de la música.

(The Moon Thieves traveling to Mali, Spain and Bolivia)

(Los Robalunas viajaron a Mali, España y Bolivia)

As Princess Marisol and Alessa pursued the Moon Thieves, they found themselves in distant lands, meeting new friends and enjoying new sounds, smells, and tastes.

La princesa Marisol y Alessa recorrieron tierras lejanas en búsqueda de los Robalunas, conocieron nuevos amigos y disfrutaron nuevos sonidos, olores y sabores.

When the music was over, they always thanked everyone for their generosity. Upon leaving, Princess Marisol would ask about the whereabouts of the Moon Thieves, but each time was given the same reply, "Ask the Wise Woman."

Cuando la música por fin dejaba de sonar, el duo daba las gracias a todos por su generosidad. Al preguntar acerca del paradero de los Robalunas, a la Princesa Marisol siempre le respondían lo mismo, "Pregúntale a la SABIA ZAMORA."

Seasons passed and at last, on the day of the Harvest Moon, Princess Marisol and Alessa wearily stumbled upon the Moon Thieves. The Moon Thieves, exhausted from many performances, were drifting in and out of sleep. Princess Marisol murmured, "excuse me," but they did not hear her. "Excuse Me," Princess Marisol said with more conviction. The Moon Thieves lazily lifted their heads from their instruments and looked at her with bleary eyes. "You have stolen the shining light of the night. Now the ocean tosses and turns and I no longer hear the moon's melodies. We must set the moon free!"

Pasaron las temporadas y por fin, el día de la luna de la cosecha, la Princesa Marisol y Alessa, ya cansadas, dieron con los Robalunas. Agotados tras tantas presentaciones musicales, ellos cabeceaban y dormitaban. La Princesa les susurró "Disculpen". No le hicieron caso. "Disculpen" repitió, esta vez con mas firmeza. Los Robalunas , con sus cabezas resposadas sobre sus instrumentos, se levantaron perezosamente y la miraron con caras de sueño. "Ustedes se robaron el brillo de la luna. Ahora el mar está agitado y revuelto, y ya no se escuchan las melodías de la luna. Debemos devolverla a su lugar!"

The remorseful Moon Thieves nodded in agreement and released the Moon, expecting it to return to its rightful place in the sky. Instead, the frightened moon dashed off and disappeared!

Los Robalunas, muy arrepentidos, asintieron e inmediatamente soltaron a la luna para que pudiera volver a su justo lugar en el firmamento. Pero en lugar de esto, la luna salió espantada y se desapareció!

The perplexed Juancho and Mato gasped and cried out, "What should we do?!" "I have heard of this woman, the Wise Zamora, perhaps she can help us, "replied Princess Marisol, "but I don't know where to find her." Suddenly, the Moon Thieves' hamster companion "El Raton," awoke and popped out from beneath Juancho's hat. "You will find the Wise Woman in the Land of Enchantment, atop the watermelon-colored mountains," squeaked El Raton.

Juancho y Mato, perplejos, preguntaron "?Qué hacemos?" "He oído hablar de una cierta mujer, la Sabia Zamora, quizás ella nos pueda ayudar contestó la princesa Marisol, 'Pero no sé donde la podemos encontrar. De repente, el ratoncito compañero de los Robalunas, "El Ratón", se despertó y asomó de debajo del sombrero de Juancho. "La Sabia Zamora se encuentra en la Tierra del Encanto, en la cima de las montañas color de sandia," chilló en Ratón.

At sunrise, the path of La Luz led them to the peak of the mountain, where they heard soft singing and humming. They found the Wise Woman perched upon a rock, singing to the birds. The Moon Thieves confessed their wrongdoings to her. "I know where the moon is;" the Wise Zamora replied "he has fled to the Village of the Moons. Use the stars to follow this map, they will lead you to him." The Wise Zamora handed a scroll to Princess Marisol, "this is for you, on this scroll is a song that you will sing to the moon so that he returns to the sky."

Al amanecer, subieron hasta la cima de la montaña por el Sendero de La Luz, donde escucharon un suave cántico y tarareo. Allí encontraron a Sabia Zamora sentada en una roca, cantándole a los pájaros. Los Robalunas le confesaron sus fechorías. "Yo sé donde está la luna;" les dijo. "Se escapó al pueblo de las Lunas. Déjense guiar por las estrellas y por este mapa: así darán con él." La Sabia Zamora le entregó un rollo de pergamino a la Princesa Marisol. "Esto es para ti. Es una canción que le debes cantar a la luna para que vuelva a elevarse al cielo."

(Princess Marisol, Alessa the Otter, the Moon Thieves, & El Raton on their journey to the (Village of the Moons).

———————————————————————

(La Princesa Marisol, Alessa la nutria, y los Robalunas en su viaje a la cima de la montaña de Sandia).

The map led Princess Marisol and the Moon Thieves to a wrought iron gate in front of an old, mysterious mansion. As they timidly went through the gate and began up the path, they saw a glowing figure of a person behind the balcony window. A shaken Princess Marisol knocked on the door, but there was no answer.

Siguiendo el mapa, la Princesa Marisol y los Robalunas llegaron ante un portón de hierro forjado, frente a una antigua y misteriosa mansión. Cruzaron el portón y recorrieron el camino con timidez. Allí vieron la figura resplandeciente de una persona detrás de la ventana del balcón. La princesa, temblorosa, golpeó a la puerta, pero nadie

Princess Marisol and the Moon Thieves entered the mansion and warily crept up a winding, creaky staircase. As they reached the landing, they saw the glowing man from the window sitting in a rocking chair. With melancholy eyes, the man watched a little girl playing on the floor. Glancing up, the little girl darted off to a darkened corner of the mansion. "We were sent by the Wise Zamora," said Princess Marisol. "I know" replied the man, "I am Metzli, and I am the Moon."

La Princesa Marisol y los Robalunas entraron a la mansión y subieron cautelosamente por una escalera de caracol que crujía con cada paso que daban. Al llegar al rellano, divisaron, sentado en una mecedora, al hombre resplandeciente de la ventana. Con ojos melancólicos, observaba a una niña que jugaba en el suelo. De repente, la niña alzó la vista y corrió precipitadamente a una oscura esquina de la mansión. "Nos envío la Sabia Zamora", dijo Marisol. "Ya lo sé" contestó el hombre. "Me llamo Metztli, soy la luna."

"Sing to him!" exclaimed the Moon Thieves. "I'm not sure that I can," Princess Marisol replied. Just then, Princess Marisol remembered what the Wise Zamora told her, "When the time is right, you will find your voice." With her confidence now sparked, Princess Marisol began singing the song written on the scroll while the Moon Thieves enthusiastically played their instruments. The Moon began to glow and to grow, and rise higher and higher, as Princess Marisol sang louder and louder.

Los Robalunas le pidieron perdón a Metzli. Sin embargo, la luna clavó la mirada fija de sus ojos grises en el cielo nocturno. La Princesa Marisol le dijo, "Tienes que regresar al cielo", pero Metzli permaneció en silencio. "¡Cántale!" gritaron los Robalunas. "No creo que pueda", contestó ella. En ese momento, recordó lo que la Sabia Zamora le había dicho, "Encontrarás tu voz cuando sea el momento indicado." Sintiéndose segura de sí misma, Marisol empezó a cantar la canción del rollo de pergamino mientras que los Robalunas tocaban sus instrumentos con mucho entusiasmo. La luna comenzó a brillar y a crecer, y se elevó más y más alto a medida que la Princesita cantaba más y más fuerte.

Princess Marisol and the Moon Thieves returned to the mountain peak and gleefully told the Wise Woman that the Moon had returned to his place in the sky. The Wise Zamora nodded knowingly, "Yes, the sky is once again filled with his beautiful melodies. Farewell Princess Marisol, forever walk with beauty." As Princess Marisol and her loyal otter strolled off into the moonlight on their way to their island home, I knew this would not be the last time our paths would meet.

La Princesa Marisol y los Robalunas regresaron a la cima de la montaña le dijeron a SABIA ZAMORA con mucha alegría que la luna ya había regresado a su debido lugar en el cielo. La SABIA ZAMORA asintió con complicidad, "Sí, en el cielo se escuchan una vez más sus lindas melodías. Adiós Princesa Marisol, camina siempre con hermosura." La Princesita y su fiel nutria de mar se fueron despreocupadamente bajo el claro de la luna, camino a su hogar en la isla. Yo sabía que esta no sería la última vez que nuestros caminos se cruzarían.

The End/Fin

Credits
Written by: Alex Paramo
Illustrated by: Audrey MacNamara-Garcia
Music by: Diplomacy of Mad Science (Matias Pizarro, Juan Carlos Ramirez)
Narrated by: Jackie Zamora

Educational Consultant Dr. Josephine "Jozi" De Leon / Translation by: Matias Pizarro Other Contributors: Christian Orellana (Peruvian track on page 13) / Juan D'Avila-Santiago (Translation Consultant) / Music tracks recorded, mixed and mastered at: The Shelter Studios, Los Angeles CA www.theshelterstudios.com / Engineered by Cesar Mejia and Marco "The Destroyer" Ruiz / Mixed by Marco Ruiz, Mastered by Cesar Mejia / Voice-over recorded at: ECA "El Caballero Aguila" Recording Studio - Valle del Sur, Albuquerque, NM. Fidel Gonzalez - azt-eca@hotmail.com / Additional tracks recorded at: James Roden Productions - Las Vegas, Nevada / James Roden - saxmanjames@gmail.com 702-205-4563

Check out our other multimedia book titles by visiting http://communitypublishing.org

More Thanks:

I would also like to thank my indefatigable Music Director, Matias Pizarro. Matias spent an incalculable amount of time bringing this project to life and I could not have done it without him. Matias, and the uber-talented Juan Carlos Ramirez, displayed an incredible loyalty and unshaken faith in this project from its inception and for that I am eternally grateful. **M**ore thanks go to our talented Illustrator Audrey McNamara-Garcia. Audrey interpreted my story in her own way and brought the characters to life in a magnificent way. **M**any more thank you's go to the inexhaustible Jackie Zamora and the gregarious Christian Orellana. Jackie lent her expertise and professionalism and breathed new life into the project during a time of uncertainty. Christian added his multitude of musical ability and his playful personality to the project. Gracias amigos!

Additional Acknowledgements:
There are so many people that need to be acknowledged and thanked that I produce this list with the fear of leaving someone out but here goes: Dr. Josephine "Jozi" De Leon, Juan D'Avila, Fidel Gonzalez, Cesar Mejia, Marco Ruiz, James Roden, Ann O'Connor, Frank Salazar Fiero, Richard Mertz, Ashleigh Abbot, Toby and Martha Sandoval, Jose "Chelo" Nunez, Sofia Zamora, Rod Lansing, Sebastian Pais, Joseph Garcia and everyone else I missed. This project has truly been a collaboration of local talent and efforts from the ground up.

Made in the USA
Coppell, TX
11 December 2024